ANISA'S International Day

Also by Reem Faruqi

Golden Girl

Unsettled

Lailah's Lunchbox

Amira's Picture Day

I Can Help

ANISA'S
International
Day

REEM FARUQI

HARPER
An Imprint of HarperCollinsPublishers

Be safe! Always cook with an adult. Don't touch sharp knives or hot stoves and ovens! And always wash your hands before and after cooking.

Library of Congress Cataloging-in-Publication Data

Names: Faruqi, Reem, author. | Jaleel, Aaliya, illustrator.
Title: Anisa's international day / Reem Faruqi ; illustrations
   by Aaliya Jaleel.
Description: First edition. | New York : Harper, [2022]
   | Audience: Ages 8–12. | Audience: Grades 4–6. |
   Summary: Inspired by preparations for her aunt's wedding,
   Anisa decides to introduce her third grade class to the art
   of mehndi for International Day. Includes recipes, activities,
   and author's note.
Identifiers: LCCN 2021063000 | ISBN 978-0-06-320623-6
   (hardcover)
Subjects: LCSH: Mehndi (Body painting)—Juvenile fiction.
   | Pakistani Americans—Juvenile fiction. | Elementary
   schools—Juvenile fiction. | CYAC: Mehndi (Body
   painting)—Fiction. | Friendship—Fiction. | Family life
   —Fiction. | Pakistani Americans—Fiction | Schools
   —Fiction. | LCGFT: Fiction.
Classification: LCC PZ7.1.F37 An 2022 | DDC 813.6 [E]
   —dc23/eng/20220510
LC record available at https://lccn.loc.gov/2021063000

Typography by Molly Fehr
22 23 24 25 26   PC/LSCH   10 9 8 7 6 5 4 3 2 1
❖
First Edition

To Zineera, Anisa, and Hanifa

All About Anisa

My name is Anisa Zakaria, and I love baking! I have my own bakery and share it with my little sister, Zineera, even though I do most of the work.

Also, I love turquoise because it's the better version of blue and green. And I like tortoises and turtles, but turtles even more, because they live in the water. I have turquoise glasses and pink glasses, but sometimes I forget to wear them or I lose them.

I love art too. Mom says that I should be a less messy artist, but I disagree. Creative people sometimes need to be messy to make beautiful art. I always try to tell Mom that, but she never understands!

I live with my family in Atlanta, Georgia. I love it when my grandparents visit or when my favorite aunt, Sana Khala, comes to see us. My parents were born in Pakistan, so some summers we travel there, which is really fun!

Contents

Chapter 1

A Package!

The doorbell rang. *DING-DONG!*

I was painting the perfect sea turtle when the loud sound made me lose my focus. My elbow knocked over my jar of brownish-green water. *Oops!*

I dumped a few paper towels over the messy kitchen table and ran to the door.

I got there just in time—a few seconds before my little sister, Zineera. *Whew!*

A package sat on the top step with our names on it. I grabbed the box first, but Zineera nudged me with a bony elbow and read the label on the box.

"It's from Nani!" she said.

I was annoyed that Zineera read the label first. But I couldn't stop smiling. I loved getting boxes from Nani in Pakistan.

The box looked big, but when I shook it up and down, it felt surprisingly light.

I tore open the box and saw my favorite color looking right back at me—turquoise!

It was a kurta! It had pink pom-poms on the sleeves and yellow tassels on the bottom.

There was also a sparkly shalwar kameez and a gold-and-blue silk gharara that Nani had sent all the way from Karachi, Pakistan.

I unfolded Nani's perfect square note.

The kurtas are for Anisa and Zineera to wear every day.
The sparkly shalwar kameezes are for Anisa and Zineera to wear to parties.

And the gharas are extra
special, for Anisa and Zineera to
wear to Sana Khala's wedding!
I wish I could be at all the
parties, but I can't wait to see you
at the wedding in a few months,
inshallah!

Zineera squealed when I took the clothes out of the box and she saw the very same clothes in her size, but in her favorite colors: pink and orange.

I dropped the box and ran to my room to admire my new turquoise kurta.

The kurta was light as paper and felt soft like my favorite turtle pajamas. The designs on the kurta reminded me of mehndi. I couldn't wait to copy them into my doodling notebook where I always save my favorite patterns and designs. My doodling notebook helps me concentrate.

What I like about mehndi is that the patterns repeat over and over. Circles go from small to large, and big paisley petals and leaves intertwine with each other.

I traced over Nani's loopy writing. Sometimes I save scraps of Nani's letters. I love her handwriting.

Then I made my way to the kitchen, where Mom was frying garlic and onions. I could hear the sound of mustard seeds popping.

Dal simmered on the stove. My mom knows how to add just the right amount of spice without making it too spicy.

"Look what Nani sent! Can I wear it to school tomorrow?" I twirled around, holding up my new kurta.

Mom looked up and smiled. She wiped her hands on her apron. Her fingertips were golden from the turmeric she'd added to the dal.

"Of course you can!" Mom said. "It'll be a nice break from the jeans and T-shirts you always wear. . . ."

Mom's eyes lingered on the table. Her fuzzy eyebrows went down when she saw the soggy paper towels. I'd forgotten to clean up the mess I'd made.

"Sorry!" I said, giving Mom my sweetest smile. "I'm an artist. Artists are creative and that means they sometimes make a mess." I hoped she would understand this time.

Usually I forget to throw away the pencil shavings from my colored pencils. And I used to forget to cap my markers, but I don't do that anymore. I love to add color to the mehndi patterns in my notebook. I find it soothing.

"Artists can be clean too! In fact, in this house, it's required," Mom said as she gave me a cleaning rag and pointed at the mess with one golden finger. She didn't put her finger down until I'd cleaned everything up.

As I balled up the soggy paper towels, I peeked over at my sea turtle. It was turquoise, like my new kurta. I decided to add some gold too.

Chapter 2

Inspiring the Class

The next morning, Mom was in a rush, so she announced that today was Anything Breakfast. I added a splash of milk to my bowl before mixing Frosted Flakes and Cinnamon Toast Crunch. Mom rolled her eyes.

I shrugged. "It's Anything Breakfast!"

Usually Mom boils us eggs. She tries to make the yolks jammy, but some days they're too hard and some days they're slimy. Sometimes they're so slimy it drips off the plate and into my lap!

After breakfast, I twirled in front of the mirror one last time. I liked how the tassels on my kurta waved at me. I couldn't wait to show my kurta off to my best friend, Katie, and my teacher, Miss Torres. Katie and I always share cookies together at lunch. Katie's mom usually makes peanut butter cookies, and Zineera and I always make sugar cookies.

If you were in third grade, Miss Torres was the teacher you wanted. Her voice was soft, even on the playground! If you got in trouble, though, her voice got even quieter, but also serious and scary.

As soon as I got to school, I rushed over to Katie so she could see my new kurta. Katie was telling Naimah a joke.

"How do we know that the ocean is friendly?

"It waves!" Katie said as she waved her hands at Naimah. Katie is from Florida.

She loves the beach.

Naimah and I both giggled. And just then Katie's mouth popped open.

"I love your dress, Anisa!"

"Thanks! It's a kurta my grandmother sent from Pakistan," I replied.

"I get boxes from my grandma too," Prerna butted in. "She sends them from India."

"Many of you need to get started on your morning work," Miss Torres said. Each morning, we're supposed to start our day in silence. When we're done with our worksheet, we get to read.

I don't think Miss Torres is a morning person.

"Anisa, I do love your new dress!" Miss Torres said.

"It's a kurta. My grandmother sent it from Pakistan!" I said proudly.

"That gives me an idea. We should have an International Day!" Miss Torres suggested as she straightened the papers she was grading.

The class buzzed with excitement.

Prerna raised her hand.

"Can we wear special clothes?" she asked.

I raised my hand.

"Can we bring in food?" I asked.

"These are all wonderful ideas! Everyone can bring in a food or an activity from a place they choose. Many of us have roots in different places in the world or from here within the United States. For the United States, please choose the state that your family has a connection to or where you have lived the longest. Or you can choose a country that you have a connection with. Please choose a place that is meaningful or interesting to you.

"Learning about each other's backgrounds can show us our differences, but it can also show us how similar we are. We can dress up too. This Friday we can create and color paper flags from around the world and hang them all over our classroom," said Miss Torres.

"And let's do International Day next Friday," she added. "Everyone can start thinking of ingenious ideas. Ingenious is our word of the week. It means clever or original. Thank you to Anisa for inspiring us!"

Miss Torres wrote *Ingenious Ideas for International Day* on the board and under-lined it two times.

My mind was already racing with ideas. Zineera and I had created what we call the A to Z Bakery—we even have a logo. (It's not a real bakery, but we do take orders from our family!) Would I bake something for International Day?

I knew I had to bring in something extra special!

Chapter 3

The Perfect Idea

The sound of sizzling oil greeted my ears when Zineera and I ran into the house after school. I couldn't wait to tell Mom about International Day. I hung my bag on the hook and ran over, stopping mid-run to stare.

Mom's favorite motia flower candle was lit. It smelled like jasmine. She only lit it when someone was coming over. Even though Mom told us to clean up all the time, our house didn't stay clean. Today, though, the house didn't look as messy as it usually did.

I peeked into the kitchen and saw Mom flipping golden-brown samosas. I dangled my fingers over the samosa plate, but Mom swatted my hand away.

"Not yet!" Mom said. "Sana Khala's coming over!"

That explained the clean house. Sana Khala is my aunt, my mother's sister.

"Mom, we're having an International Day at school! Miss Torres liked my kurta and it gave her the idea to ask everyone to bring in a food or an activity from their country or state. And we get to dress up!" I said.

"You should bring sugar cookies," Zineera said.

"It has to be something from Pakistan," I explained.

"But *you're* from Pakistan," said Zineera.

"It's not the same!" I rubbed my fuzzy caterpillar eyebrows as I thought.

I got out my turquoise feather pen and doodling notebook. I wrote *Ingenious Ideas for International Day*. I liked that ingenious was a fancy word for clever. But the delicious smell of the samosas kept distracting me.

I made my eyes big and my mouth really sad as I looked at the pile of steaming samosas. Mom saw my sad face, put the spatula down, and handed me the tiniest samosa on the plate.

The samosa had the perfect crunch and burst of flavor. It almost made up for the fact that I knew Sana Khala was going to get married soon and move forty-five minutes away from us. I was really going to miss having her drop by last minute for tea. Luckily for me, she was coming over more to plan her wedding that was a few months away. In the meantime, there were lots of parties for her! Whenever Sana Khala came over, Mom made Zineera and me chai too. Ours had extra milk, and honey instead of sugar.

I nibbled as I thought about the perfect food to bring in.

"Can I have another?" I asked.

"Me too!" Zineera added.

Mom gave us a look that meant NO, just as the doorbell rang.

DING-DONG!

Sana Khala was here! I ran over to answer the door, beating Zineera to it.

Sana Khala lifted Zineera off her feet into a hug. Then she hugged me too and swung me around. She smelled like roses and vanilla mixed up. I like to draw the sparkly hijabs Sana Khala wears. Today, she was wearing a shiny purple one with a lavender dress and turquoise nail polish on her fingers and toes. Since Baba wasn't home, she unwrapped her hijab before rearranging her hair into a big bun.

What I love about Sana Khala is how she always plays board games with us and how she reads out and explains the instructions of a new game to us. Mom always makes us read the instructions ourselves and figure them out, which sometimes makes Zineera and me argue. Sana Khala always explains the instructions in a way that we understand.

Sana Khala is a Montessori teacher, and

whenever she makes play dough for her class, she also makes us big containers of homemade play dough. She always mixes the blue and green food coloring in the play dough to make turquoise play dough for me.

"I hope this isn't too last minute, but can the A to Z Bakery make some thumbprint jelly cookies for my dholki tomorrow night that my friends are throwing for me?" she asked as she danced on tiptoe. It looked like she was bobbing up and down, twirling her wrists into small circles. The dholki is a wedding party for Sana Khala's friends, to sing and dance. Mom joined in and started to clap and sing an Urdu song.

I rolled my eyes.

I ran to the kitchen and brought Sana Khala the menu form that Zineera and I had made for orders. "Just let me know how many cookies you want for the party! We take last-minute orders too!"

Zineera bounced around. Whenever Zineera was excited, she didn't walk. She bounced and hopped. Zineera usually asked for two ponytails when Mom did her hair. At the beginning of the day, they would start high, and by the end of the day, they were a lot lower. As she bounced, her ponytails flew in the air. Right now, since she was bouncing so much, they were really low and drooped.

We always used Zineera's thumb to make a circle in the dough, since it was smaller. The cookies had just the right amount of sticky sweetness in the middle. We knew they were Sana Khala's favorite dessert. They reminded her of the cookies she used to buy in Pakistan. But it was still fun to give her the menu. I couldn't wait to get started on our order! I started to calculate the ingredients we needed, just like a professional baker would.

"Smells amazing in here!" Sana Khala said as she followed us to the kitchen. She plucked a samosa from the pile and popped it into her mouth. The oil made her glossed lips even shinier. I never understood how Sana Khala always wore lipstick or lip gloss and could eat delicious oily things without messing up her makeup. I also didn't understand how Sana Khala ate almost everything with ketchup. This time, she was dipping her second samosa into ketchup that Mom had put out just for her. When her samosa was finished, Sana Khala licked the ketchup off her fingers before adding another squirt of ketchup to her plate and reaching for more samosas.

"Mmmm! Who doesn't love samosas?" she said.

And then it hit me. My ingenious idea. I knew exactly what I would bring to class for International Day! Samosas!

Chapter 4

A Big Problem

Even though I was wearing a turtle shirt and jeans instead of my turquoise kurta, I felt light as I skipped to my classroom. I couldn't wait to share my ingenious idea with my class!

Sometimes when I was bored in class, I doodled on my jeans. That's what made these jeans my favorite ones.

As I walked in, I overheard Katie telling Jason a joke. "Why do people swim at salt-water beaches?"

"Why?" he asked.

"Because a pepperwater beach would

make them sneeze!" Katie pretended to swim and sneeze at the same time.

I giggled. I loved how silly my best friend was.

Miss Torres frowned at us behind her glasses. Her soft voice got quiet and serious.

"You can choose to play now, but then you won't be playing at recess."

I didn't want my best friend to get me in trouble! I've never missed recess, so I quickly wiped my smile off my face and sat down. Whenever someone was going to miss recess, Miss Torres would write their name on the whiteboard under *No Recess*. Everybody stared at that person—I definitely did not want to be them. Katie had missed recess a couple of times by joking around and talking during silent time. I sighed with relief when Katie sat down too. She was still smiling.

"Attention, wonderful writers! If you haven't chosen a country or state yet, I'll be happy to help," said Miss Torres, pointing to her world map. "Now, who would like to share their ingenious idea for International Day?" asked Miss Torres as she uncapped a fat orange marker.

Many hands went high up in the air.

Miss Torres wrote Katie's name first.

"I would like to bring in crepes. My great-grandmother was French—"

"If you're French, you should bring in French fries!" Jason joked.

Miss Torres shook her head. "As a matter of fact, some say French fries originate from Belgium."

"I want to bring in crepes and Nutella. Nutella is from Italy, actually," Katie said.

Everyone liked Nutella, so Miss Torres

had to ask for silence.

"My grandmother is Mexican," Miss Torres said, "and I'd like to bring in empanadas. They're usually savory but sometimes they can be sweet. I'll stuff them with fruit for dessert. My grandmother is from Mexico City and she bakes us beef empanadas whenever we visit her. She uses the leftover dough to make sweet empanadas with apple filling and adds sugar, cinnamon, and cloves. When I was little, she would sneak me an extra one when my parents weren't looking. I thought my parents didn't notice, but my mom says she did; she just didn't say anything." Miss Torres smiled as she wrote *empanadas* next to her name.

Miss Torres is going to love samosas! I thought as I waved my hand back and forth. *Samosas are yummy—they're stuffed with meat or vegetables!*

Miss Torres looked my way.

"Me! Me!" I said with a big smile. I stood up and waved both arms.

Miss Torres pushed her glasses up and raised both of her eyebrows extra high and scary. *Oops!* I hoped she wouldn't write my name under *No Recess* on the whiteboard for being too loud.

I sat back down, face serious, and raised one hand, quietly this time.

Miss Torres chose Prerna instead.

"I'm going to bring samosas!" Prerna said proudly.

My mouth popped open.

Prerna continued, "My parents are Indian and it's a food we eat at home. They are stuffed pastries. My mom fills them with vegetables. They look like this. . . ." She made a little triangle with her hands and then rubbed her tummy.

Everyone laughed.

Everyone except me.

"Sounds delicious!" said Miss Torres as she wrote *samosas* next to Prerna's name.

I, Anisa Zakaria, am a creative person. I have ingenious ideas. And creative people don't copy each other.

So I quickly put my hand down.

I looked at my desk and rubbed my eyebrows.

"Anisa, what about you?" asked Miss Torres.

I opened my mouth, but no words came out.

"Um . . . I know I want to do Pakistan, but I'm still deciding what to bring . . . ," I answered.

"Are you sure?" asked Miss Torres.

I wasn't sure, but I nodded anyway. I couldn't reach my doodling notebook, so I drew tiny flowers on my jeans instead.

Miss Torres moved on to Azusa. She was going to bring in origami paper to fold into cranes for an activity. Her mother was from Japan. Naimah was going to bring in pilau. Her grandfather was from Kenya. Ciel's family had lived in Georgia for a long time. She was going to bring in pecan pie that her grandmother bakes. Jason was going to bring in New York–style pizza since he's from New York, and was going to wear his New York hoodie. Everyone's name had a food or an activity next to it. My name looked sad and lonely on the chart.

My shoulders sagged.

It was *not* a super day in third grade.

Chapter 5

An Idea Right Under My Nose

I didn't look at Prerna for the rest of the day. When Katie and Naimah asked me again at lunch what I was bringing, I tried to change the subject by sharing my star-shaped sugar cookies with them.

On the bus ride home, Zineera talked all about her day, but I couldn't stop thinking about International Day and how I didn't have an idea. Aren't creative people supposed to be full of ideas? When I got home, there were no samosas frying and no scented candles either. Instead, there were three large trash bags by the door. It was trash day tomorrow. My mood matched the trash—foul. I dumped my book bag on the floor. *WHAP!*

Mom frowned and pointed at the book-bag hook. Her eyes looked extra big, outlined in black kajal. She wasn't wearing her glasses.

Zineera must have had a great day in first grade, because she couldn't stop talking about it. She was hopping around the kitchen, going round and round in circles. I wished she would just freeze and be calm, but Zineera didn't seem to like being calm much. I rolled my eyes and shoved my bag on the hook.

"Anisa, did your manners fly away?" asked Mom.

Questions like that make me annoyed. My feet stomped in response.

"Well?" asked Mom.

"Prerna's bringing samosas for International Day," I mumbled.

"So?" Zineera said. "We can still make samosas!"

I groaned. "It's boring for two people to bring the same thing!"

"Says who?" asked Mom.

"I can't copy people!" I explained. "I must be original. I need an ingenious idea."

"Not everyone can be creative all the time. You'll figure it out, inshallah. You always do." Mom sighed. "Plus, it would be tricky to make samosas for a whole class right now." Mom pointed to a colorful pile of roses that she was making into a garland for Sana Khala. "I'm not even done yet. . . . Now you both need to start baking! It's Sana Khala's dhoki tonight!"

"So that's why you're wearing your contact lenses! I forgot it was tonight!" I said.

Baking always makes me feel better.

And just like that, International Day floated out of my mind.

I washed my hands and reached for the ingredients. In the beginning, Zineera and I would take a long time baking an order. But we're pretty quick now. As I cracked eggs carefully and measured ingredients, Mom helped Zineera turn on the electric mixer. Once the dough was mixed and felt just right, I whipped out my cookie cutters. I loved shaping the dough into different designs. I chose the heart cookie cutter the most for Sana Khala. Then Zineera got out the strawberry jelly and made thumbprints while I scooped jelly into them.

"High five?" asked Zineera, waving her sticky hand. Her thumb was all doughy, and she had a dot of flour on her forehead.

"Nope!" I giggled.

Mom used to have an annoying rule that

if we baked, we had to be like ghosts and leave no evidence of our baking. The first time we heard that, Zineera and I started yelling, "Oooh! Spooky!" while we cleaned. So now Mom tells us to be invisible instead. It should look like no one has baked.

While Mom helped us put the cookies in the oven, we quickly wiped the counters and put the ingredients away. When the timer went off, the cookies were golden-brown perfection!

Mom rushed over to take the cookies out of the oven, with her makeup and shiny kurta on and her polka-dot pajamas peeking out. It was funny to see Mom halfway dressed. Zineera and I packed our cookies in a cardboard box with a sticker of our logo on it that I had printed out myself.

I ran upstairs to get dressed in the sparkly shalwar kameez that Nani had sent for the dholki. Nani was so excited Sana Khala was getting married, she had bought us clothes for her wedding months ago, even before she knew when the wedding date was! I love how Pakistani clothes always have unexpected colors together. This one had an orange kurta and a teal shalwar. The dupatta was tie-dyed teal and orange. I made a note to remember to use those colors in a painting.

I spun around the room in excitement before finding my hairbrush underneath a pile of books. I grabbed a matching hair tie from the floor and handed it over to Mom. I hoped Mom wouldn't notice that I hadn't *really* brushed my hair. Even though Mom brushed my hair extra hard to get rid of the knots (she noticed!) and braided my hair tightly, I didn't complain like I usually did. Instead, I gazed at my hands. I couldn't wait for them to be decorated with flowery mehndi designs.

"One more thing!" Mom plucked a few left-over flowers from the garland pile and added them to my braid. Now I really looked ready!

At the dholki, my heart beat fast with the beat of the drums and the singing. Small candles flickered, and glittery streamers twinkled in every corner of the room. Sana Khala's friends had gone all out with decorations! My eyes felt like they were smiling as I looked around the room to see all the colorful clothes. Girls were wearing hot pink and purple, gold and royal blue, silver and maroon, and every color combination of the rainbow. I wished I could paint everything I saw.

I looked around for Sana Khala. At first I didn't recognize her in a shimmery gold sari and heavy gold jewelry. I wondered if it was really her. She was wearing a big teeka on her forehead that really made her look like a bride. Garlands of marigolds dangled all around her and were pulled aside so they looked like curtains. She was sitting on a silky orange sofa, which was on a stage decorated with fat red cushions. I wanted to go up to her, but I felt shy. Zineera, though, was bouncing on the sofa and telling her all about our cookies.

I kept staring at Sana Khala. She must have noticed, because a second later she stuck out her tongue.

I giggled. Mom handed me her garland made of roses and told me to put it on Sana Khala. The garland of roses smelled amazing. I carefully put it around Sana Khala's dupatta, then proudly handed her our box of cookies.

"Delicious!" she said as she popped two whole cookies into her mouth. Her lipstick still looked perfect. I was a little relieved that she never ate ketchup with her cookies. I placed the box on the dessert table.

Zineera and I high-fived. We loved it when our customers were satisfied.

"I hope you're ready to get your mehndi done!" Sana Khala said. She showed me where to sit. White sheets were spread on the floor, with colorful cylinder cushions to sit on while we waited to get our mehndi done. I love how fresh mehndi smells—like earthy leaves. There's no smell like it!

As I waited in line, I remembered how, when I was small, Nani would make her own mehndi. She'd put a dollop of mehndi on my palms and let me clap my hands together. It made two messy circles on my palms. But today, I was looking forward to getting a fancy design done by a professional.

I opened my palms wide and tried not to move when Muna Aunty started to work. (Muna Aunty isn't my actual aunt, but we call all of Mom's friends aunty.) I loved how neatly she held the green cone and drew delicate swirls and curly flowers. It's different from how you hold a pencil. Muna Aunty drew flowers in seconds. I couldn't wait to copy the designs into my doodling notebook.

"Can you draw a turtle too?" I asked.

Muna Aunty paused for a second, thought about it, then drew a tiny turtle in the middle of my palm. I bounced with joy.

"Sit still or it'll smudge!" said Muna Aunty, squeezing the mehndi cone.

I nodded and widened my palms as

much as I could. I was too big to mess up my hands and have smudgy palms. Even though the mehndi was cold and wet, I felt cozy and warm inside. Looking down at the intricate designs, I felt all grown up.

Just then, my smaller cousin, Ishaq, ran by us, leaping over cushions. When he saw my mehndi, he held his nose. "Gross!"

"Why are you even here? This is a party *for girls*!" I yelled.

Ishaq pretended to gag before running back upstairs. I sat as still as possible and opened my palms wider.

"How's school?" Muna Aunty asked.

Suddenly I didn't feel warm anymore.

"We're having an International Day and someone else is bringing in samosas, which was *my* idea."

Muna Aunty nodded as she drew.

"I wanted my idea to be unique. Ingenious. Most of the class is bringing food, so

I was thinking that maybe I should bring in an activity instead. Azusa's mom is from Japan, and she's bringing origami. But I still don't have any ideas."

"Don't worry!" Muna Aunty reassured me. "You'll work it out. Sometimes a good idea is right under your nose. . . . Next, please!"

I shuffled away so that Zineera could have a turn.

"Finally!" whooped Zineera as she plonked herself on the cushion. I didn't think Zineera would be able to sit still without smudging her mehndi. I hoped I would be happily surprised.

I put my hands close to my face and inhaled the fresh smell. I remembered what Muna Aunty had said. A good idea *was* right under my nose! I felt tingly all over.

I had the perfect activity for International Day!

Chapter 6

More Trouble

Today, Mom woke up early to make boiled eggs. Just my luck!

"Assalamualaikum!" she greeted me as I walked into the kitchen. She placed an egg onto my plate.

"Wa-alaikum-as-salam," I mumbled. I was still sleepy from the dholki and wished we could have had Anything Breakfast instead.

I peeled my egg and sliced into it. It wasn't hard or slimy. The golden yolk stuck gently to the egg white. I must have looked surprised, because Mom explained, "Seven

minutes seems to be the magic number for boiling eggs!"

"And for a Friday treat, breakfast dessert, doughnuts," Baba said, coming into the room and taking a box from behind his back. Baba always joked that we had two stomachs, one for food and one for dessert. Baba patted his tummy before taking a big bite of a maple-frosted doughnut.

I quickly ate my egg and moved on to my chocolate-frosted doughnut.

"Look!" I held out my hands.

"Beautiful!" said Baba.

Baba said the same thing to Zineera, who'd started on her strawberry-frosted doughnut, even though her mehndi designs were a little smudged because she hadn't waited long enough for her mehndi to dry before using her hands.

"Everyone needs to get in the car NOW!" ordered Mom. "All this double breakfast eating and late-night partying is making you late!"

Zineera and I rushed to the car. I had to tell her to wipe the frosting off her chin. On the way to school, I traced my mehndi designs. My turtle had already turned a deep chocolate brown, almost as dark as the chocolate frosting.

I couldn't wait to show Katie and the rest of the class my hands, and to have my activity written down next to my name on the classroom chart. The halls were quiet, which meant the bell had already rung. Oops! I hurried down the hall.

When I rushed into the classroom, I noticed everyone had already started their morning work. I cleared my throat, hung up my book bag, and opened my palms wide as I walked over to show Katie.

"Morning work needs to be done in

silence," reminded Miss Torres.

I frowned. I didn't think I could wait until lunch to show Katie. *I'll just quietly show her,* I thought. I opened my palms wider and walked closer to Katie. I did a small wave, but I wasn't sure if she saw me.

Just as I reached Katie, she turned to Ciel and whispered. Then Katie pointed to her palms, looked up, and both of them laughed.

Usually I love how funny Katie is, but this time her laugh made my stomach feel funny. It felt like Katie was laughing at my mehndi. I closed my palms into fists.

"Do you want to hear a joke?" Katie whispered.

I shook my head. I wasn't smiling.

Miss Torres frowned at us behind her round zebra-print glasses. "Silence means silence."

My cheeks felt warm. I hid my hands under my desk. My pencil felt heavy when I started to work on my subtraction, and I couldn't focus.

I can't believe it. Katie doesn't like my mehndi! My head drooped.

Maybe mehndi isn't an ingenious idea for International Day after all. . . .

Chapter 7

Survey Time

"Attention, marvelous mathematicians!" Miss Torres said. "Let's talk about surveys. A survey is when you gather information or data. We can use this data to make a graph. Surveys can help you make good choices. For example, when I bring in my empanadas for International Day, should I stuff them with bananas or apples?"

I hate the taste and smell of bananas, and how mushy they are. My bakery will bake anything with fruit, except banana bread. *Yuck!*

Choosing a Filling

Apples Pros 🙂	Apples Cons 🙁
• firm • crisp	• seeds • sour

Bananas Pros 🙂	Bananas Cons 🙁
• quiet to eat	• mushy • slip on a peel

Miss Torres wrote *Choosing a Filling* as her title.

"First, what are some pros and cons of bananas and apples? Remember, pros are the positives, the things that you like, and cons are the negatives, things that you don't like."

"One con is that apples have seeds that you can accidentally eat. It's happened to me," said Ciel.

"A pro is that apples are firm and crisp. They're not mushy and disgusting like bananas. Bananas have lots of cons," I said.

"A pro is that bananas are nice and quiet to eat, unlike apples!" said Azusa, covering her ears.

"A con is that apples can be sour," added Naimah.

"A con is that you can slip on a banana peel. Bananas are dangerous!" said Jason.

"Looks like we have different opinions!

Let's collect data by voting," said Miss
Torres.

Miss Torres wrote *Bananas* on one side
of the board and *Apples* on the other. When
Miss Torres said bananas, I kept my hand
way down. When she said apples, my spir-
its lifted, and I waved my hand high.

As Miss Torres counted votes, Prerna
whispered, "I like your mehndi!"

My stomach felt a little better. I opened my palms wider to show Prerna the designs.

I whispered, "I think Katie doesn't like my mehndi. She laughed at it. . . ."

Prerna gasped. She opened her mouth to say something, but just then Miss Torres spoke.

"Thank you, marvelous mathematicians! According to the data we collected, I should use my grandmother's recipe and stuff my pastries with apples," said Miss Torres. "Speaking of food, it's time for lunch!"

My stomach started to feel funny again. Would Katie want to sit with me at lunch? What if she thought my mehndi was gross, like Ishaq did? I didn't care what he thought, but I cared what Katie thought.

I looked at the survey and sighed. I wanted International Day to be perfect. Maybe if I made a chart, it would help me too?

Chapter 8

A Good Friend

In the cafeteria, I sat next to Naimah instead of Katie. I tried not to look her way, because I didn't want her to make fun of me again. Instead of coming over to check why I wasn't sitting with her, Katie sat right next to Ciel. For lunch, I had spaghetti—usually Katie laughed when I showed off, sticking a noodle in between my top two teeth. But Naimah didn't laugh. I peeked at Katie. Ciel wasn't making her laugh either.

I tried to listen as Naimah talked. But having your best friend nearby but not sitting with you felt weird. I always sat with

Katie. Usually I liked Mom's spaghetti, but this time I only had a few bites. Even though Katie was only a few seats away, it felt like she was six hundred seats away. My shoulders slumped forward. Although the cafeteria was warm, I felt cold all over. I closed my almost-full spaghetti thermos and put it away.

Is Katie even my friend anymore? I stared at the designs on my hands, wishing they could give me an answer.

"Your hands are so pretty!" Azusa said.

I started to feel warm again.

"I love the turtle!" added Naimah.

"I wanted to bring in mehndi for International Day," I said quietly.

Azusa clapped. A couple of girls cheered. "Wow! That would be amazing!" Azusa said.

"But Katie made fun of Anisa's mehndi!" said Prerna.

"I mean, I think she did . . . ," I whispered. But no one heard me.

My side of the table got quiet. My classmates looked sorry for me. It made me feel worse instead of better.

Katie was now laughing with Ciel.

I took out my turquoise feather pen and my doodling notebook from my lunch box. I take my feather pen and notebook almost everywhere I go. It helps me focus. At that moment, I needed it for some math.

"I'm taking a survey. How do you know someone is a good friend?"

I titled my list *A Good Friend.*

"A good friend shouldn't get you in trouble," said Azusa.

"A good friend should listen to you and like your ideas," added Naimah.

"A good friend needs to be kind. Being kind is better than being funny," Prerna said, looking at Katie.

"I don't choose friends. They choose me!" added Jason.

"Good friends share their cookies!" added Azusa.

I looked down the table at Katie and wondered if I should share my sugar cookies with her like I usually did. She was already sharing her peanut butter cookies with Ciel. I looked down at my data.

A Good Friend

- Shouldn't get you in trouble
- Should listen to you and like your ideas
- Should be kind (more important than being funny)
- Should choose you
- Should share cookies

Katie didn't follow Miss Torres's silence rule in the mornings.

Katie didn't listen to me when I tried to show her my mehndi.

She laughed at me. (At least I think she did.)

Katie chose to sit next to Ciel, when she could have sat next to me.

Katie didn't share her cookies with me today.

I put a question mark next to the first thing on my list. I put an X next to the next four.

A Good Friend

- Shouldn't get you in trouble ?
- Should listen to you and like your ideas X
- Should be kind (more important than being funny) X
- Should choose you X
- Should share cookies X

In baking, you had to have the correct ingredients. Once when Zineera and I had made chocolate chip cookies, Zineera had put in baking powder instead of baking soda. Our cookies were all flat and sunken in. We made sure to not make that mistake again. When you bake, you need to pay attention and to make sure you're adding the correct ingredient, and the right amount of it.

It seemed like Katie just didn't have the right ingredients to be a good friend.

Chapter 9

The Big Mistake!

After lunch, I felt better about my palms, and at recess, I showed Miss Torres my hands. Her smile got big when she saw the turtle.

"I want to bring in mehndi for International Day!" I said.

"What an ingenious idea, Anisa! I'll add it to the chart," replied Miss Torres.

I skipped over to the monkey bars to play with Prerna, Azusa, and Naimah.

Katie joined us.

"Why didn't you sit with me at lunch? Do

you want to hear another beach joke?" she asked.

I gave Katie the coldest look I could.

"I collected some data today, like Miss Torres taught us, and I've concluded that you're not a good friend."

Katie's mouth turned down and she made her face innocent.

This made me madder than I already was.

"Do you have anything to say?" I asked. My voice sounded like someone else was speaking.

Katie's mouth trembled.

"I didn't think so," I added.

I felt a little of my anger evaporate when I saw Katie's face, but I quickly turned away to swing on the monkey bars. I didn't want to start feeling sorry for her. Who needed a best friend anyway?

But the monkey bars didn't feel as swingy as I thought they would.

After recess, it was time to make our flags. Miss Torres had put out colored construction paper, glue, and scissors. Miss Torres said we could talk softly using our inside voices. Katie wasn't sharing any jokes and she wasn't working on her flag.

Her head was down on her desk and she didn't even have her paper out. Normally I would have checked on her, but she wasn't my best friend anymore. Although I had my green and white paper for the Pakistan flag, I didn't feel like cutting or gluing either. My heart beat fast when I heard Miss Torres call Katie over. I picked up my scissors and kept my eyes very focused on making a white crescent moon for my flag.

"Anisa," Miss Torres called, in a serious voice. Her voice was extra quiet.

I walked over super slowly as everyone stared.

"Katie says you collected data to decide if you should be her friend?" asked Miss Torres.

I pointed to my palms. My words felt hot. "Katie made fun of my mehndi. But best friends aren't supposed to make fun of each other, right?"

"I never made fun of you!" said Katie.

"I saw you in the morning talking to Ciel about me! You were laughing and pointing at your hands," I replied.

Miss Torres looked around the room. "Ciel . . ."

Ciel's eyes widened. She looked afraid.

Katie looked confused.

I was confused too. Was it possible that I had misunderstood?

"We were laughing in the morning because Katie had told me a joke," Ciel whispered.

"A joke about me!" I huffed.

"No. The joke was, 'What kind of tree fits in your hand? A palm tree!'" explained Ciel.

"I see," said Miss Torres.

My mouth dropped open.

I'd made a big mistake!

Chapter 10

Apology of Action

Everyone looked at me. I looked down at the floor.

My throat felt tight. Even though I'm taller than Katie, I felt very small all of a sudden.

"Anisa, do you have something to say?" Miss Torres said.

"I'm sorry," I whispered.

"Next time, don't be so quick to assume something about a friend! Surveys are great for things like math and empanada flavors. But they're not a tool that anyone

should use to judge a friendship. I want you to think about an apology of action. Find a way to say sorry to Katie that involves doing something kind for her. Got it?"

I nodded.

"It's okay, Anisa," said Katie. "I like your mehndi. I want some on International Day too."

Katie's voice was kind and she gave me a tiny smile. I felt tears poke my eyes, but I quickly blinked them away with three strong blinks. I was the bad friend, not her! I tried to smile at Katie, but it felt like my lips didn't know how to smile anymore.

I remembered that when Zineera and I fought, Mom and Baba would also make us apologize by doing something kind for the other person. For Zineera, I would make a card or play dolls with her, but I wanted something extra special for Katie.

As Katie and I walked back to our seats, my feet felt heavy. I wondered if Katie felt the same.

Katie didn't have her head down at her desk anymore. She was getting her construction paper out, which made me feel a little better. I quickly finished my flag and reached for my notebook and turquoise feather pen and started to make a list of what Katie liked.

I needed an ingenious idea for an apology of action. I was going to make my apology special because Katie wasn't just any friend. She was my best friend.

When I closed my notebook with a snap, I felt a little lighter. I felt like a cookie that was just beginning to rise.

International Day

On the morning of International Day, instead of feeling excited, I felt nervous. Sometimes when I waited for my cookies to finish baking in the oven, I felt excited as each minute got closer to the timer buzzing. This time, as each minute got closer to school starting, I just felt nervous. I wore my turquoise kurta, but I didn't swirl in front of the mirror. All I could think of was Katie and if she would accept my apology of action.

"Are you excited about International Day?" asked Zineera in the car. "You're so lucky! I wish first grade had International Day too!"

Instead of answering, I nodded and looked out the window. Zineera saw my face and got quiet too. Since it was morning, her ponytails were really high. They looked cheerful, unlike me.

At school, the class buzzed with excitement. Everyone except me. The smell of delicious food was in the air, but I didn't feel hungry.

"Do you have your apology of action?" asked Azusa. She was wearing a purple kimono.

"Katie's over there!" pointed Prerna. She was wearing a blue-and-gold gharara.

I wanted to tell them I liked their clothes, but my mouth felt dry as flour.

Will Katie like my apology of action? I wondered. My stomach churned like cookie dough in my electric mixer.

Mom sat at a table with a fat green mehndi cone. She'd drawn a few designs for my class to choose from. I'd designed a secret drawing for Katie that I told Mom to keep facedown.

As a line started to gather around the table, I found my voice.

"I would like Katie to go first," I said. Then I turned my secret design over.

For my apology of action, I'd customized a mehndi design just for her. I'd drawn a dolphin and swirly waves on a piece of paper, and the letters BFF riding the waves.

Katie gasped when she saw the design.

"I love it!" she said, and she hugged me. The hug made the worries in my stomach stop churning.

Mom copied my design neatly onto Katie's palms. I reminded Katie to hold still so that her design wouldn't smudge. Even Miss Torres got in line for mehndi! Ciel got a cloud design since her name means sky in French. Prerna chose a circular flower design on her hand, while Azusa chose a spiral design.

"Can I get my name on my arm?" asked Jason.

"Sure!" said Mom.

Mom wrote Jason's name and did a small geometric design of triangles around his name.

Jason flexed his arm muscles before saying thanks.

When it was Miss Torres's turn, she liked her mehndi so much she got two hands done. She looked a little funny with her two arms outstretched and had to get Jason to help her hold her clipboard.

Looking around, I admired all the colorful clothes my friends were wearing. Prerna's gharara swayed when she walked. Naimah was wearing a colorful Kenyan kitenge that was hot pink and orange, with a wide matching hair band. Katie was wearing a red shirt and shoes that her grandmother had bought her from a French boutique last year. When everyone's hands were dry, we folded paper to make Azusa's origami cranes. I loved Azusa's flowy sleeves and the way they moved as she folded paper neatly.

Finally it was time for food. Miss Torres only had to call us once. *International Day is the best!* It was exciting to not have to eat lunch out of a lunch box. Our garland of flags dangled over the food table, making our food look extra appetizing and colorful. I loved how my Pakistani flag's crescent and star twinkled back at me.

Prerna's samosas were stacked high like a tower on a fancy red plate. Naimah's pilau was heaped in a silver foil tray and felt like it had just been taken out of the oven. Jason's New York–style pizza's cheese stretched extra far when Katie and I got a yummy slice. Miss Torres had arranged the food so the dessert empanadas, Ciel's pecan pie, and Katie's Nutella crepes were at the end of the line. When I sat down by Katie, we were so busy eating, we didn't have time to talk.

When Miss Torres came over with her camera, Katie and I immediately held out our mehndi palms next to each other. We put our other arms around each other's shoulders. Miss Torres did not need to tell us to smile.

"Beautiful!" said Miss Torres. She took another photo, zooming in on our hands.

My turtle and Katie's dolphin looked like they were floating together. They looked like best friends.

Just like Katie and me.

Glossary

assalamualaikum: Muslim greeting that means "peace and blessings be upon you"

chai: Urdu word for *tea*

dal: lentils

dholki: a Pakistani ceremony in which, traditionally, women gather to sing, beat drums, dance, and apply mehndi to celebrate an upcoming wedding

dupatta: a light shawl Pakistani girls and women wear over their shalwar kameez. It can be draped over the head or chest.

empanada: a baked or fried turnover made of pastry and filling. It is usually savory, filled with meat, or it can be sweet, filled with fruit as a dessert. It's commonly eaten in Southern Europe, Mexico, Latin America, Indonesia, and the Philippines.

gharara: a women's garment consisting of a kurta, a dupatta scarf, and wide-legged pants that flare dramatically from the knees. Girls and women wear them on fancy occasions.

hijab: a headscarf Muslim girls and women may wear

inshallah: "God willing"

kajal: a powdery eyeliner that some Pakistani women wear

khala: maternal aunt, meaning your mother's sister

kimono: national dress of Japan, a robe with flowy sleeves

kitenge: a colorful piece of fabric used as a dress, headscarf, or baby sling in Africa

kurta: a flowy tunic top worn by people in regions of South Asia, such as Pakistan

mehndi: henna paste that temporarily dyes hands, usually drawn on hands to celebrate events

motia: an Arabian jasmine flower

nani: maternal grandmother, your mother's mother

origami: the art of paper folding, associated with Japanese culture

sari: an outfit that South Asian women wear that is made of several yards of lightweight cloth. It's draped so that one end makes a skirt and the other is typically a shoulder covering.

shalwar kameez: a traditional dress worn by women and men in Pakistan. The top, or kameez, is usually loose. The pants are usually wide on the legs but cuffed at the bottom.

teeka: jewelry, usually worn by brides,

that is pinned to their hair and dangles on their forehead

Urdu: Pakistani language

wa-alaikum-as-salaam: the return greeting for assalamualaikum. It means "peace and blessings be upon you too."

Recipes

Samosas

(Makes 20 samosas)
- 1 pound ground beef
- 1 teaspoon cumin powder
- 1 teaspoon ground coriander
- ½ teaspoon turmeric powder
- ½ teaspoon black pepper
- 1 teaspoon salt
- 1 teaspoon garlic
- 1 teaspoon ginger
- ½ teaspoon chili powder (depending on your taste!)
- spring roll wrappers (buy at grocery store)

- 2 to 3 tablespoons flour
- water
- vegetable oil for frying

1. Mix the beef and spices. Have an adult help you brown the seasoned ground beef with the above spices.
2. Wrap the ground beef in spring roll wrappers. Try to make neat triangles using the method on the next page.
3. Mix the flour with just enough water to make a thick paste for sealing the samosa triangles.
4. Shallow fry your samosas in vegetable oil, with an adult's help.

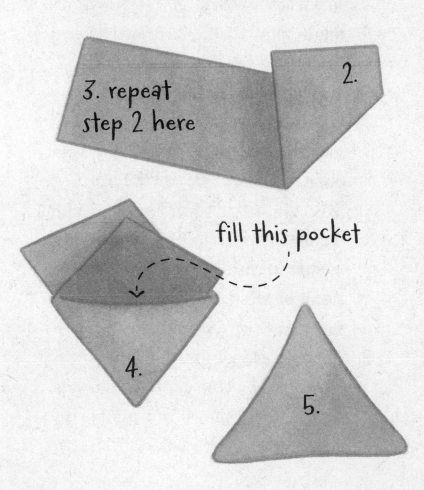

1.

2.

3. repeat step 2 here

fill this pocket

4.

5.

Thumbprint Cookies

(Makes 36 cookies)

- 2 sticks of butter or 1 cup, melted in microwave in 20-second increments
- 1 cup sugar
- 3 eggs
- 1½ teaspoons vanilla extract
- ½ teaspoon salt
- 3½ cups all-purpose flour
- 2 teaspoons baking powder
- jam or jelly in your favorite flavor

1. Preheat oven to 375°F. Dump everything except the jam or jelly into a bowl. Mix or knead together with hands or electric mixer.
2. Shape cookies and place on an ungreased baking sheet two inches apart. Then press a thumbprint shape into each cookie. Using a

small spoon, fill each thumbprint with jam or jelly.

3. Place cookies in preheated oven for ten minutes. (Be sure to have an adult help you place cookies in oven and take them out of the oven.)

4. The bottom of the cookies should be pale brown when they are finished. Cool on rack before serving. Be sure to have an adult help you place cookies in oven and take them out of the oven.

Activities

All About Mehndi

Mehndi, or henna (the Arabic word for mehndi), comes from a henna plant with the Latin name *Lawsonia inermis*. The leaves are ground to make a fine powder, and then a paste is made. After the mehndi has been applied to your hands, it usually takes about thirty to forty-five minutes to dry. People usually leave it on their skin for three to eight hours, to allow the stains to darken, before washing it off. Some people sleep with it on so that the color is darker.

The mehndi color on skin lasts for a week to ten days. Mehndi cones can be bought from a halal meat store or a Pakistani or Indian store. Make sure to buy natural mehndi. Do not buy black mehndi, as it can contain chemicals and can cause an allergic reaction. Always test mehndi and do a patch test on your skin first before applying it.

Happy designing!

Anisa's Mehndi Turtle Design

Katie's Dolphin Design

Design a Logo

The A to Z Bakery logo looks like this:

Do you want to run a business?

What would your logo look like?

Draw it here!

Make a Flag Garland

You'll need:

- construction paper
- scissors
- markers or colored pencils
- atlas or any reference that shows the flags of four countries
- glue (optional)
- tape
- string

1. Cut your construction paper into quarters.
2. Copy the flags of four countries, or design your own flags for imaginary countries. If you like, add to your flags by cutting shapes out of construction paper and gluing the pieces onto your flags.
3. Tape your completed flags to the string.

4. Hang your garland on the wall.

Can you name all the countries you made?

Author's Note

I have two daughters named Anisa and Zineera who, like the main characters in this book, love to bake. They too call their home bakery the A to Z Bakery. I also have a Sana Khala, who I call Khalajee. When I was a child, she made the best play dough, and she always read us the instructions from brand-new and difficult board games.

Like Miss Torres, when I was a teacher, I implemented that my students do an "apology of action" when they needed to apologize, because they would be more sincere in apologizing. Also, Miss Torres is a real and favorite teacher of my children.

I love my home country of Pakistan and enjoy celebrating it any chance I get. I hope Anisa's story inspires you to have an International Day, to celebrate each other's similarities and differences, and to make sure that you are being the friend that you would like to have.

Acknowledgments

A huge thank-you to:

My editor, Alyson Day, for believing in Anisa, championing her, and publishing our story!

My agent, Rena Rossner, for guidance, enthusiasm, and for your passion at all times!

Eva Lynch-Comer for all your work and making Anisa and me look good on book jackets!

The dedicated HarperCollins team— production editor: Shona McCarthy, marketing director: Emma Meyer, publicist: Samantha Brown, and production manager: Kristen Eckhardt.

Aaliya Jaleel for bringing Anisa to life and to Molly Fehr for nailing yet another gorgeous cover!

My SCBWI critique partners, who are always there for me to offer encouragement, tweaks, and critiques: Melissa Miles, Keith Resseau, Amy Board, Vicki Wilson, and my first family readers: Sana Dossul, Huma Faruqi, and Fatima Zakaria (who asked for more!)

Maleeha Siddiqui for your beautiful blurb and friendship.

Jamilah Thompkins-Bigelow and Ashley Franklin for clarity and support.

My *entire* family, and special shout-out to Farah and James Van Valkenburg, Marina and Mazhar Rizvi, Zarina Zakaria (Nana!), and Josefina Bautista for being loyal readers, and Zaheer Faruqi for always buying my books!

Dr. Amena Dossul and Asna Dossul for your love of turtles and baking for inspiration.

Dr. Firasat and Nazia Malik, Ismat Malik (Daado!), Naoman Malik, Hamzah, Talha, and Osman Faruqi for everything.

To the original Zineera and Anisa, and one day Hanifa, inshallah, thank you for always enjoying and proofreading my stories!

My eleventh-grade English teacher, Mrs. Patricia Dobbs Carman, for making me a better writer.

All my writing friends and authors who help me boost my voice, including Dr. Salma Stoman, Sarah Stoman, Aya Khalil, Saadia Faruqi, Marzieh Abbas, Becky Sayler, and Rena's Renegades.

Librarians, bloggers, authors, and educators for championing my stories and getting them into classrooms and into the hands of your students. It means the world! Special shout-out to #MGBookChat, #BookPosse, #BookExcursion, #BookAllies, #BookSojourn, #LitReviewCrew, Mrs. Ghazala Nizami, Dr. Gayatri Sethi, Shifa Saltagi Safadi, Kirin Nabi, and Mr. John Schu.

Author Debbi Michiko Florence, whose Jasmine Toguchi series my daughters and I fell in love with and inspired me to keep trying!